Oh No, Peedie Peebles!

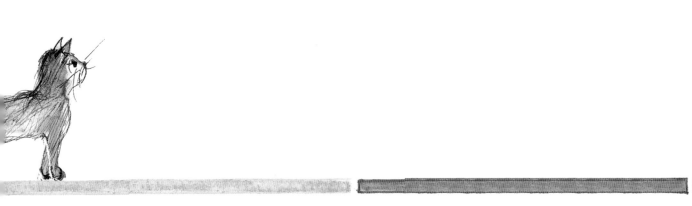

Oh No, Peedie Peebles!

Text and illustrations by Mairi Hedderwick

BIRLINN

This edition published in 2011 by
Birlinn Limited
West Newington House
10 Newington Road
Edinburgh
EH9 1QS

First published in 1994 by Random House Children's Books

www.birlinn.co.uk

ISBN: 978 1 78027 002 9

British Library Cataloguing-in-Publication Data
A catalogue record for this book is available from
the British Library

Page make-up by Mark Blackadder
Printed and bound in China

For Sophie

The Peebles family have just moved house. There's a lot of work to be done; the new house is very dull and dingy inside.

'Just needs a coat of paint, that's all,' they said.
Peedie Peebles went to find his paint brush.

'Peedie Peebles is *not* allowed to go near any
of the paint pots,' said Mum and Dad and big sister Bo.

Peedie Peebles was annoyed.

The hall was the first room to be painted. 'I like red,' said Mum.

'So does Peedie Peebles,' smiled the postie. 'Oh no, Peedie Peebles!'

The second room was the kitchen.
'I like yellow,' said Bo.

'So does Peedie Peebles,' laughed the milkman.
'Oh no, Peedie Peebles!'

The third room was the bathroom. 'I like blue,' said Dad.

'So does Peedie Peebles,' warned the bin man. 'Oh no, Peedie Peebles!'

The fourth room to be painted was the sitting room.
'I like orange,' said Mum.

'So does Peedie Peebles,' noticed the nosy neighbour.
'Oh no, Peedie Peebles!'

Mum and Dad's bedroom was the fifth room.
'We love green,' they said.

'So does Peedie Peebles,' said the nice neighbour.
'Oh no, Peedie Peebles!'

The sixth room to be painted belonged to Bo.
'I love purple,' she said.

'I'm tired,' said Mum. 'Only one room left,' said Dad.
'The last room to do is Peedie Peebles'.'

But Peedie Peebles' bedroom was *already* painted.

'I don't like this,' said Mum.
'Look at the mess,' said Dad. 'Oh *no*, Peedie Peebles!'

With a bit of help, Peedie Peebles' room was soon finished.

It was the best painted room in the whole house.
'Time for a bath,' said Mum.

'OH NO, Peedie Peebles . . . !'